Tell me some more..

Tell me
some more..

Story by CROSBY NEWELL BONSALL
Pictures by FRITZ SIEBEL

An I CAN READ Book®

■ HarperCollins*Publishers*

Library of Congress catalog card number: 61-5773
ISBN 0-06-020601-2 (lib. bdg.)

For my husband

"I know a place,"
said Andrew to Tim,
"if I tell you,
will you believe me?"

"I will believe you," said Tim,

"I will believe you.

Tell me and see."

"I know a place," said Andrew,
"where I can hold an elephant
under my arm."

"The trunk and all?" Tim said.

"The trunk and all," said Andrew.

9

"And I can hold a camel
in my hand.
If I use two hands,
I can hold two camels.
Maybe three."

Tim said, "Three camels
in your two hands?"

"It's true," Andrew said.

"Tell me some more," said Tim.

"In this place I can pat a lion,"
Andrew said.

"On the nose?" Tim asked.

"On the nose," said Andrew,

"and I can scratch his ear."

"He won't bite you?" Tim asked.

"Oh, no," Andrew said,

"he won't bite me."

"Tell me some more," said Tim.

"In this place I can
tickle a seal," Andrew said.

"I can even take the seal home.

I can put the seal

in my father's chair."

"On your father's lap?" asked Tim.

"Maybe," said Andrew.

"Tell me some more," said Tim.

"In this place," said Andrew,
"I can be taller than a tree,
bigger than a ship,
wider than a whale."

"Can you be fatter than a moose?"
Tim asked.

"In this place I can be,"
said Andrew.

"Tell me some more," said Tim.

"In this place," said Andrew,
"I can pick up a river
and never get wet at all."

"Is there a fish in the river?"
Tim asked.

"There might be," said Andrew.

"There might be a boat in the river.

And a man in the boat.

And a sea gull sitting on a wave."

"Tell me some more," said Tim.

"In this place," said Andrew,

"there are mountains and fountains,

and moons and spoons,

and rings and kings,

and clocks and socks,

and stairs and chairs,

and pigs and wigs,

and hens and pens,

and drakes and lakes,

and trucks and bucks,

and oodles and oodles

of poodles."

"Is there a star there?" Tim asked.

Andrew said,
"There is a sky full of stars."

"And a rainbow, too?" Tim asked.

"Oh, yes, there's a rainbow, too,"
Andrew said.

"Is everything there?" Tim asked.

Andrew said, "Yes, everything."

"A camel in your hand
and *everything?*" Tim said.

"Yes, yes, yes," Andrew said.

"I don't believe it," said Tim.

"It's true," Andrew said.

"Did you see it
with your own two eyes?"
Tim asked.

"With my own two eyes,"
Andrew said.

"Where?" said Tim.

Andrew said, "I won't tell you.
You won't believe me."

"I will believe you," said Tim,

"I will believe you.

Tell me and see."

"No," Andrew said, "I will show you.
I will take you there."

Tim followed Andrew.

Around the corner,

across the street,

past the candy store,

up the steps,

through a door,

27

into a big quiet room.

A big quiet room

with books along

every wall.

"Is this the place?" Tim asked.

"This is the place," Andrew said.

"Where is the camel?" Tim asked.

Andrew said, "It's here."

"I'll find it," said Tim.

But it was not in the closet.

It was not in the drawer.

It was not in the inkwell.

It was not on the floor.

Was it under the desk?

On top of the table?

Behind the door?

Stuck on a label?

No.

Tim looked all around the room. "I know," he shouted.

Andrew said, "S-s-sh."

"But I know where the camel is," whispered Tim.

"Show me," said Andrew.

Tim walked away.

Andrew waited.

In a minute Tim came back.

Tim came back

and put a camel

in Andrew's hand.

"See?" Tim said. "I told you

I could find the camel.

I found the camel

right here in this book.

It was the only place

that camel could be."

Andrew gave the book back to Tim.

It was a big book.

There were pictures of camels

in the book.

And stories about camels.

"Look," said Tim, "I'm holding

a lot of camels in my hand."

"What did I tell you?" said Andrew.

"I think I'll take home a rocket,"
Tim said, "and a steam shovel,
and one giraffe."
Tim picked out a book.
He picked out another book.
And another book.
Then he was ready to go.

Andrew said, "Wait a minute.

I'll take a book home, too."

Tim waited.

Then Andrew and Tim walked back

through the doors,

down the steps,

past the candy store,

across the street,

around the corner.

Andrew and Tim,

a rocket,

a steam shovel,

and one giraffe.

And Andrew carried an elephant

under his arm.

"Be careful," said Tim,

"or my giraffe may stick out his neck

and stop all the cars

from here to the hill.

He may stop all the cars

one after another. It may take us

all day to get home."

Andrew said, "Who cares?"

"We will ride home on my elephant.

He is big. He is strong.

He will carry us home."

"Can he carry a rocket,

a steam shovel, and me?" asked Tim.

"Sure," said Andrew,

"and one giraffe, too."

Tim said, "Or I may fly in my rocket

right to my house. I may land

in my own back yard.

Boy, will my mother be surprised!

My mother will say, 'Timothy,

take that rocket out of this yard.

My garden is a mess.

Timothy, did you hear me?'

That is what my mother will say."

Andrew said, "If I ride home
on this elephant, my mother will say,
'This house is not big enough
for all of us and an elephant, too.
You will have to keep him outside.
Outside! Outside!
Outside with that elephant!'
Then what will I do?"
asked Andrew.

"We might build a cage in the yard,"
Tim said,

"in the yard between your house
and my house."

And Andrew said,

"Then we use the steam shovel.

We scoop up the rocket.

Scoop up the elephant.

Scoop up the giraffe,

and put them all in the cage.

My mother won't mind that."

"My mother will," said Tim.

"Hey, we're home," said Andrew.

He stopped at his gate.

"Now do you believe me?"

said Andrew.

"Believe what?" said Tim.

"You know what," said Andrew.

He went in his house.

Tim walked next door.

Tansy sat on the front step.

Tim's sister Tansy. He put the books behind his back.

"Guess what I have in my hands," he said.

"A bread and jelly sandwich," said Tansy.

"Guess again," Tim said.

"A cricket," said Tansy.

Tim said, "No, you will never guess. Here in my hands I have a rocket, a steam shovel, and one giraffe."

"Oh, pooh," said Tansy.

"It's true," said Tim.

Then he sat down beside Tansy.

"I know a place,"

said Tim to Tansy,

"if I tell you,

will you believe me?"

"I will believe you," Tansy said.

"Tell me and see."

"I know a place," said Tim

"where I can hold an elephant

under my arm."

"The trunk and all?" Tansy asked.

"The trunk and all," said Tim.

"Tell me some more," said Tansy.

"No," said Tim.

"You won't believe me."

"I will believe you," said Tansy.

"Tell me and see."

"No," said Tim, "I will show you.
I will take you there."